The ADHD Vampire

Matthew Vaughn

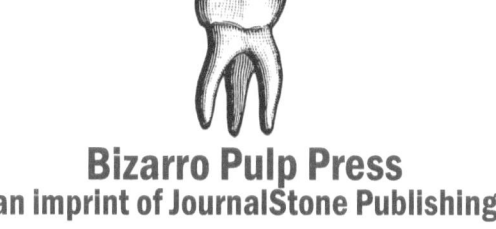

Bizarro Pulp Press
an imprint of JournalStone Publishing

Bizarro Pulp Press books may be ordered through booksellers or by contacting:

Bizarro Pulp Press, a JournalStone imprint
    www.BizarroPulpPress.com

    ISBN: 978-1-940161-98-3

Printed in the United States of America
JournalStone rev. date: January 2, 2015

    Cover Art: P.A. Douglas
    Interior Formatting by: Lori Michelle
        www.theauthorsalley.com

1.

Sixty-two year old Estelle headed down to the lower level of the cruise ship for her scheduled rendezvous with sixty-nine year old Ralph. She was hoping he was going to fuck the shit out of her. As old as they were, they didn't have time for love making; they just needed to fuck while they still could. Besides, she had already given him a hand job under the table at dinner. It was time for him to return the favor.

She slowly shuffled along in what would have been complete silence if it weren't for the random squeak from one of the wheels on her walker.

Estelle shivered as she walked. There didn't seem to be any heat on the lower level. Ralph had told her to meet him in the cargo hold. She was sure that's where she was, and she squinted while trying to make out some of the objects around her. She was pretty sure they were crates, but there wasn't any sign of Ralph.

"Hey, sexy momma," Ralph said. He stood next to a short but wide crate to her left. She walked past him without seeing or hearing him. Ralph watched her go by as a short series of farts escaped her rear. She laughed a little and he shook his head.

"Estelle! Hey, Estelle!" Ralph said. He walked up behind her, his hip giving him pains from how fast he was moving. He put a hand on her shoulder and she screamed. She swung around with her walker in her hands, ready to attack.

"Oh my God, Ralph! You scared me something awful!" she said. She used her right hand to massage her chest.

"Geez, Estelle. I'm sorry. I wasn't trying to give you a heart attack or nothing."

"Well, you almost did. What were you thinking sneaking up on a helpless old lady?"

"I wasn't sneaking. I yelled at you, ya old... wait. Never mind that." Ralph took the hand that was on her chest and brought it down to his crotch. "I took a Viagra and it's already kicking in."

Estelle giggled and tightened her hand on Ralph's hard member through his pants.

"Well, well, let's not waste any time. We're not getting any younger, are we?" she said.

"You want to take out your teeth and gum on my cock a little?"

"You've already had your turn, mister," Estelle said as she turned away from him. "It's my turn, and I like it from behind."

She pushed her walker up against the short crate. With no ceremony, she dropped her bloomers and pulled off her adult diaper. Ralph stared at the wrinkly, saggy ass in front of him and shuddered. He closed his eyes and pictured Olivia Newton-John bent over in front of him, with her tight, sweet ass poked out at him. His pants became restricted, so he dropped them to his feet and scooted up behind Estelle.

"I may be old, but I can still take a good pounding," she said. "So let's not be gentle, okay?"

Ralph took to pounding her ass as much as he could with his bad hip. He was pretty sure it was enough for her, the way she whooped and hollered. She held onto her walker, and it smacked into the crate repeatedly, in rhythm with Ralph's thrusts. The sound echoed through the dark level of the ship. Ralph was a little paranoid that someone was going to hear, but not enough to stop.

"My plumbing was taken out years ago, so don't bother with pulling out," she said. Ralph could feel himself getting ready to go, so he began thrusting harder, going as deep as he could possibly go. Estelle cried out in pleasure as Ralph thrusted one final time. His hip made a loud cracking sound and Estelle farted on his stomach. Ralph's dick slid out of Estelle as he fell to the ground, both from pain and from gagging on her fart.

"Sorry about that, honey. It happens sometimes when I get excited," she said. She bent over and picked up her diaper as another wet fart leaked out.

"That's not a big deal, but I threw my hip out there in the end . . . " Ralph stopped and cocked his head like a dog. "What's that sound?"

Estelle saw her walker vibrating. She pulled it away from the short crate and it stopped.

"I think it's coming from this box here," she said, backing away from it.

They both watched the crate closely. At first, it didn't do anything. Estelle thought that maybe she was just seeing things, as she was getting up there in years. Maybe she was becoming delusional, she thought.

Matthew Vaughn

A loud bang came from inside the crate, causing Estelle to let out a scream and drop her diaper. She went to grab her walker for support and knocked it over. It smacked the side of the crate on the way down.

"Hello?" a voice from inside the crate said.

"Estelle, there's somebody in there!" Ralph said. He climbed up to the crate and put his ear against the lid. "Hello? Hey, are you okay in there?"

"Yes, I'm okay," the voice said. "I seem to be stuck. I could use some help getting out of this thing."

"Hold on buddy, we'll get you out of there!" Ralph said to the crate. He took a quick look around the cargo hold. His eyes may not have been the best anymore, but he spotted a blurry object nearby he thought could be a tool box.

"I'm going to see if I can find something to help this poor feller out. Talk to him, Estelle, and try to keep him calm."

"Okay," Estelle said. Her voice was a little shaky, but she leaned onto the crate and talked gently. "Hello in there. Just stay calm, we're getting you out."

"Tell me, are we in America yet? Have we docked in New York? The city of lights, and dreams, and the one that never sleeps?" the voice asked.

"Uh, New York? This is a senior's cruise," Estelle said. "We've been out for seventeen days and now we're on our way back."

"What? That little rat-faced man promised me this boat was going to New York!" The crate shook with a pounding from inside. "I never would have paid that little bastard to load me onto this ship if I had known!"

"I found something, Estelle!" Ralph yelled. He

8

held up a crowbar in one hand and rubbed on his sore hip with the other. The walk over to the toolbox had been torture for Ralph, and he wasn't looking forward to walking back, but he hadn't survived two tours in Vietnam and seen action in Grenada just to puss out like this in the end of his years.

Estelle watched Ralph as he winced and limped back her way. She turned back to the crate.

"Are you saying you had someone put you in that crate?" she asked.

"Yes, and I was supposed to sleep until we reached our destination, then I would be awoken."

"Why would you do something like that to yourself?" she asked. She backed away from the crate, unsure of what was happening.

"All right, let's get this sucker open!" Ralph said. He had come behind Estelle and startled her when he spoke.

"Wait a minute, Ralph," she said to him. He either ignored her or was too focused on his mission. He walked up and shoved the crowbar into the slight separation between the crate and the lid. He put all his weight onto the crowbar and the nails in the crate gave some.

"Ralph, something's not right here, I don't know about this," Estelle said. Again, Ralph shoved the crowbar under the lid and pried. He still wasn't listening to Estelle.

It took about four more good pries on the lid and a force from inside lifted the lid from the crate. The separation was so violent that it knocked both Estelle and Ralph onto their asses.

Estelle let out a startled noise as she witnessed a man sitting upright in the crate, dirt falling from his body. He turned and looked at the old couple.

Matthew Vaughn

"I am Horace Dracul. You have awakened me from my slumber," he said. He pulled himself up from the crate and brushed the remaining dirt off. "You will pay for this mistake with your blood!"

Ralph scooted away from the crate, his bad hip causing him to drag his left leg on the ground. Estelle stood her ground; Horace had her hypnotized with his stare. He climbed completely out of the wooden box and made his way toward her. She swayed in place but was unable to move. Horace closed the distance between himself and Estelle. She leaned her head to the left and exposed her neck, inviting him. He reached out and put one hand on her shoulder, the other on her head. He pulled on her head to the point where the tendons in her neck were stretched to their limit, and then bared his fangs.

Something moved in Horace's peripherals. Distracted, he looked up to see Ralph scooting backward along the floor trying to get away. Instantly, he dropped Estelle, her old frame falling to the ground, and went for the elderly man.

Ralph screamed.

Horace gripped Ralph's shirt and lifted the retired war veteran high into the air.

Ralph tried kicking his feet, but it caused the pain in his hip to become even more horrendous. Ralph decided he was too old, so he decided not to fight the inevitable.

There was a loud smacking sound that got Horace's attention. Distracted again, Horace turned his head and saw Estelle trying to pick up the walker. Horace let go of Ralph, who landed with a painful thud.

Horace went to scoop Estelle from the ground,

and Ralph cried out while trying to adjust his misaligned back.

Just as suddenly as Horace had turned to Estelle, he turned back to Ralph.

Horace took three steps toward Ralph, then he stopped and stared at the floor. Something shiny was near his foot. It sparkled when the light hit it a certain way. Horace reached down to pick it up.

Estelle let out a wet fart that was followed by foul-smelling diarrhea. Horace turned from the shiny object and looked at her.

"I have spared you this long, but now you are mine!" Horace said. He tried his best to sound tough and scary.

Estelle still held her diaper in her hands. She lifted it toward her face, gripping it tightly, as Horace approached.

The only time Ralph had ever been this scared was in Vietnam. One particularly bad time was when his platoon was ambushed, he was terrified. Charlie was ready to kill him, until luck would have it, another squad showed up and took them out. Now, he was so scared he wanted to give up and die, but he would be dishonoring the brave men that saved his ass if he did that. He felt old and weak, unable to fight off this madman, but he couldn't let Estelle die by his hands. "Oh God, just kill me and get it over with!" Ralph shouted from behind Horace.

Again, Horace turned away from the terrified Estelle and advanced on Ralph. A dark stain appeared on the front of Ralph's pants as his courage quickly faded. Horace grabbed the old man by the ankle and lifted him up from the floor. Ralph hung there, upside down and suffering agonizing pain from his back. His piss ran down his chest and off his shoulder. It dripped down and landed on Horace's boot. Horace looked down, following the sound of the piss. He stared at it as it dropped onto his boot, one drip after another.

Something clacked against the floor, and Horace turned to see Estelle's shit-covered ass sticking up in the air. She was on her hands and knees, attempting to stand. Her dentures had fallen out and hit the floor.

Horace let go of Ralph without a second thought, his mind now only on Estelle. When Ralph hit the floor, he screamed out in pain again. This time Horace hadn't yet stepped away from Ralph. He turned back to the old man, who now twisted on the ground with his hands on his lower back.

Horace snatched Ralph up from the floor again, and this time he finally succeeded in sinking his teeth into Ralph's neck. He sucked on his blood until he got overly-excited and ripped a huge chunk of meat from Ralph's neck with his teeth. The act of doing this slung massive amounts of blood around. Horace hated to waste all that sweet, sweet juice, but if it was true what the woman had said about this being a cruise ship, he could afford to.

With blood all around his mouth and down the front of his shirt, Horace turned to Estelle and overtook her as she began to scream. This time he was focused and drank from her veins until he was satisfied.

2.

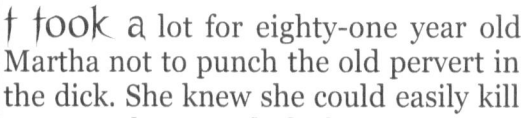t took a lot for eighty-one year old Martha not to punch the old pervert in the dick. She knew she could easily kill the man with one punch. Instead, she listened to him politely for a few minutes.

"I'm just saying, momma, you can't be a day over sixty with that sweet body of yours," the perv said. He leaned up against the wall with his arms crossed in front of him. He was trying to be smooth; unfortunately, he had a couple features going against him. The main issues were his bald, sun spotted head and the loose, flabby, shirtless belly hanging over his Hawaiian swim trunks. That look just didn't do it for Martha.

"My wife, she's probably off with her dentures locked around some poor bastard's cock, so we've got plenty of time to fuck for as long as the Viagra will let me."

"I appreciate the, uh, flattering words, but I'm not interested," Martha said.

"Oh, I think if you got a little taste you'd be very interested," the perv said. He grinned widely, and Martha saw his hand grab his crotch and adjust his erection through his bright colored swim trunks.

That was all Martha could take.

She stuck her foot out and kicked the man's right foot, the one that supported all his weight. He went down fast, barely getting a yelp out. He hit the floor hard, and Martha was already walking away by the time his boney ass struck carpet.

Martha smiled. She was on this senior's cruise for the same reason as everybody else—to unwind and have some adult fun—but she couldn't stand it when someone acted slimy and creepy while they hit on her.

She knew she had to control herself. Her body was strong enough to kill a man easily. At one time she worked for The Company. They trained her body and mind, as well as enhanced her body with various cybernetics. She was a super intelligent, government-built killing machine, but that was before. She was retired now, just an ex-spy looking to get a little frisky and have some fun on a cruise.

Rounding the corner that led into the dining room, Martha almost ran directly into a younger fellow dressed as part of the ship's crew.

"Whoa, sorry. Excuse me, ma'am," the young man said to her.

"That's okay, just as much my fault as yours," Martha said with a smile.

"I hope you're enjoying your stay on the U.S.S. Exciter, ma'am," the young man said. "My name is First Mate Ryan. Let me know if there is anything I can do for you."

"Thank you very much," she said, smiling again. "Everything has been quite lovely so far."

Two old ladies walked up on the pair, interrupting their conversation.

"Excuse me, sonny. Did I hear you say you're the

first mate?" one of the old ladies asked Ryan. Martha checked out the woman's white hair and thought it looked almost blue. A very unflattering hair style.

"Yes ma'am, First Mate Ryan. Is there something I can help you with?"

"Yes, I haven't seen my husband, Ralph, since earlier," the woman with the blue hair said. "Around dinner time, I think."

"And my sister Estelle, she's been gone for a long time, too," the other old lady said.

First Mate Ryan looked past the ladies to Martha. They shared a knowing glance. Estelle and Ralph had probably gone off together and found themselves a nice quiet place to get busy.

"It's only been a couple hours since dinner," Ryan said, trying to reassure them. "I'm sure they will turn up shortly,"

"Ralph needs to take his heart pills," blue hair said. She had a worried look on her face and she wrung her hands while she spoke. "He always remembers to come and take them on time."

Martha didn't realize at first how upset the woman was, and it made her wonder if something did happen to her husband. But the ship's crew was perfectly capable of locating a couple of missing passengers. They could handle this. She was retired; she didn't save people and fight bad guys anymore. Besides, she had a date with the captain coming up.

She walked away from Ryan and the old ladies.

***

Upstairs, in his private quarters, the captain was having after-dinner wine with seventy-three year old Delilah. The captain himself was only fifty-four, but he had always had a thing for older women. His mother's thirty-nine year old friend had taken his virginity when he was thirteen, and ever since then, he was drawn to older women.

"More wine, my dear?" he said. His plan to get her drunk and in bed with him before his rendezvous with eighty-one year old Martha was going smoothly.

"Just a smidge more, dear. I'm already feeling a little loopy," Delilah said. The captain smiled as he topped off her glass.

"Well then, by all means, feel free to lay back and make yourself comfortable."

Delilah giggled into her wine glass.

"You're a bad boy, Captain," she said. She set her wine glass down and leaned back onto his bed. The captain's smile grew along with the bulge in his pants.

Without warning, the door swung open and Delilah let out a startled scream. Ryan, the first mate, burst into the room.

"Captain!" He stopped when he noticed Delilah on the bed. His cheeks turned red and he looked up to the ceiling. "I'm sorry to interrupt, sir."

"What is the meaning of this, Ryan?" the captain said, standing up angrily.

"We found something in the cargo hold you need to see," Ryan said.

"Well, can't you see I'm a little pre-occupied? What is it that I *need to see*, as you put it?"

"Uh, I'd rather not say, sir." Ryan glanced over at Delilah. "It would be better if you saw it for yourself."

The captain helped Delilah to her feet and then checked his watch. He could still juggle his time with these ladies and make it work, if this didn't take too long.

"My dear, you're more than welcome to remain

here until I return." He said to Delilah, and then looked at Ryan. "This had better not take too long."

3.

Playing the guitar wasn't as easy for Stephen as he made his way to the ripe old age of sixty-three, which would be in just another week. The years of playing semi-professionally had really taken its toll on his hands, causing bad arthritis to plague him throughout the day. He was sure the chronic masturbation didn't help either.

Walking through the bowels of the cruise ship, Stephen lifted his Takamine acoustic guitar from where it hung at his side. He situated it across his torso and began to strum the chords to Metroplis's *The Darkest Side of Night*.

Stephen closed his eyes and thought of J.J. He always thought of her when he played that song; it was one of her favorites. Playing that tune almost guaranteed she was going to take her clothes off. But that was a long time ago. He figured she was just as old and wrinkly as he was now. He didn't even know if he would want to fuck her again. All he could picture was her sucking his brother's cock, and he hated that mother fucker. He was content with playing the song and reliving the memories in his head.

The ADHD Vampire

Stephen opened his eyes and jumped when he saw a person standing in front of him, half covered in shadows.

"You play very well," Horace said. "I can play a little guitar too."

"Uh, okay," Stephen said. He knew that was supposed to be his cue to offer his guitar to this guy—he's had it happen to him many times before. But, Stephen loved that guitar, and he didn't like for anyone else to touch it.

Horace took two steps towards Stephen and out of the shadows. The overhead light illuminated his blood-drenched chin and upper body. Stephen handed his guitar to him without another word.

"It's been a little while since I've played," Horace said. He plucked at the low E string and listened, making sure it was in tune. As he listened his eyes wandered up toward the ceiling, staring off into space as he plucked the next string, then the next.

Many, many years ago, there was a pretty, young music teacher; Horace remembered now. Surprisingly, for all his flaws, Horace picked up playing music exceptionally fast. With all the time he spent alongside the music teacher, he fell in love with her. He wanted to turn her into a vampire so they could live together forever. But, every time they would get together for lessons, he would get lost in playing, or tuning instruments, or staring at the many bright and shiny things around. Then, his brother, Vlad, would show up and mesmerize her into going away with him. Horace knew Vlad was feeding on her, and probably other things. One day, Horace was able to keep his distractions at bay, and he told the music teacher his plans. She flipped out and went screaming into the arms of Vlad, who took the opportunity to feast on her again. This time he drained her, to Horace's dismay.

Looking down at the guitar, Horace realized that his mind may have wandered and given the owner of the instrument time to escape.

Stephen did use Horace's starring off into space as a chance to run, but instead of going back to the stairs and making his way to higher decks, he hid behind some nearby equipment.

Horace walked slowly, the guitar still in hand. There were many motors and mechanical equipment along the walkway. He found himself being drawn to the whirling gauges and valves that let out bursts of stem. One panel had dancing lights, and Horace's eyes traced imaginary patterns that only he could see.

A noise from behind pulled him from his wonder and he turned, throwing the guitar out, headstock first. There was Stephen, now with a guitar sticking out from his chest. Blood ran down the smooth side of the neck.

Horace moved up to the man, the guitar impaling him and stuck into the wall behind him. Horace reached up with his left hand and wrapped his fingers around the guitar's neck, and used his right to pluck the strings. He smiled at the sound of the beautiful instrument, and then he began to feed on Stephen's blood.

4.

he captain, his first mate Ryan, and a couple other crew members stared down at the bloody remains of Ralph.

"What in the hell could have done this?" the captain asked.

"It looks like an animal of some kind, sir," Ryan said.

"I know what it looks like, but there aren't any animals on board." The captain scratched his head. "At least there shouldn't be. We need to check the cargo hold and make sure we don't have something on board that shouldn't be."

"Sir, we also found this over here," one of the other crew members said. They walked over to where the man stood. There was an open crate and blood nearby it on the floor.

"What the hell was in that crate?" the captain asked.

"It looks like it was opened, maybe by this old guy on the floor," one crew member said. "But there couldn't have been any animals in there. Nothing could survive inside a sealed crate."

"Vince, I need you to check the manifest and see

what was in that crate," the captain said to the crew man. "This has to stay quiet. I don't want the passengers to get all riled up. Someone clean up this mess, I have some business to take care of."

The captain left the crew in the cargo hold and went on to continue with his evening.

5

In the main corridor that led to the passenger cabins, sixty–three year old Rachelle scooted along, trying to make it to her cabin before she shit herself. Rachelle had been having some difficulty holding her bowel movements, yet she couldn't force herself to go through with the indignity of wearing diapers. It was bad enough she needed to cart around an oxygen tank, she didn't need any other handicaps holding her back.

She could see her door, the sixth one down on the left, and began to feel hopeful she was going to make it. A small fart escaped from her ass cheeks and she looked behind her to see if anyone may have heard. No one was there. When she turned back around a man was standing down the hall. Rachelle could tell he was a young man, but he wasn't dressed like any of the crew men. She hadn't heard any of the other ladies mention bringing any young lovers aboard.

Rachelle hoped he wouldn't try and talk to her. She didn't want to be rude, but she really had to get to the bathroom.

She watched the man as she reached her cabin door. He never moved. She pulled the key card out of her pocket and looked back one last time before unlocking the door. The man was gone. She looked down the way she had just come; nothing. He must have gone into one of the cabins when she wasn't looking.

Rachelle inserted the key card into the lock and pushed on the door once she heard the click.

She screamed out as two arms wrap around her from behind, causing her to let go of the handle of her oxygen tank. As she was forced into the cabin, the nasal cannula that was wrapped around her ears and under her nose tightened as it pulled the oxygen tank behind her.

Once inside the cabin, Horace let go of Rachelle. He heard the tank clank across the ground. He turned and saw the shiny metal cylinder; it appeared to him as the most fascinating thing he had ever seen. He picked the container up, completely forgetting about his prey. She realized instantly that his attention was elsewhere and made a run for it.

Rachelle managed maybe two feet before the tubing of the nasal cannula went taut and pulled her head back, her feet running out from underneath her. Rachelle slammed onto her back, the wind knocked out from her stomach.

The tubes that supplied her with oxygen to keep her alive had betrayed her.

The sound of her hitting the floor grabbed Horace's attention. She was able to suck in just enough breath to scream.

The man stepped into her view; he looked very familiar to her. Rachelle squinted her eyes. Had her eye sight really gotten that bad? Finally, she felt she could make out the man, it was Chester, her grandson. He had turned into to such a handsome young man, which was good cause he was one ugly, awkward looking child.

"Chester dear, what are you doing here?" she asked. "Did you see the man who grabbed me? Did you scare him off and stop him from hurting me?"

"I don't know who this Chester is. I am Horace Dracul."

"Your voice sounds really weird Chester, you sound a little queer." She tried to shake her head, but nothing wanted to move for her. "I know my son Patrick will be really disappointed if you turned out queer."

"What are you talking about? I'm not this Chester person, I told you that. My name is Horace."

"Oh, dear, is Horace your boyfriend?" Rachelle tried to stand up and look for the other man Chester was talking about, but she couldn't. An awful pain had crept into her body. She was becoming terrified.

"Listen you stupid woman. My name is Horace, and I don't know who Chester is. Even if I did he would just be another victim." He stopped, realizing what he was saying. "Just like you."

Horace pounced on her and bit down on her neck. Rachelle felt relieved, she wanted desperately to escape the pain. As Horace fed, she closed her eyes. She could see her dead husband Stan waiting for her at the end of a bright tunnel. She smiled as she passed on.

***

Martha watched the two old ladies sitting at the bar in the lounge; they were making out. They shared a stool, one wrinkly old chick sitting on the other wrinkly old chick's lap, their faces smashed into one another as they explored each other's mouths with their tongues. The woman on top, the smaller of the two, had her hands on her girlfriend's head as she ground her hips against her. The one on the bottom had her hands on the smaller one's ass.

For some reason, the sight of these two geriatric lesbians reminded Martha of 1954. The last time she saw her one true love alive.

She was fresh out of her parents' house and had moved into a place with her lover, Trish. Of course, back then they had to pretend they were just roommates. Behind closed doors they were lesbian lovers going to town on one another every chance they got, using homemade sex toys; who wanted to be seen trying to buy the real thing?

The two decided to attend a party Trish had been invited to by some co-workers. It was a field party, with lots of drinking and dancing. Cars had been parked strategically so that headlights could be used to illuminate the gathering. The vehicles created a circle and lit the makeshift dance floor at the center. Speakers blared rock n roll, swing, and rockabilly. Bill Haley and His Comets's "(We're Gonna) Rock Around the Clock" blared through multiple car stereos.

Martha had pulled Trish out onto the dance circle on that song, their favorite. The two women were quite intoxicated. Toward the end of the number, Martha, drunk and lost in the moment, leaned in and kissed Trish on the lips.

"What are you doing?" Trish asked, pulling away from Martha.

"What? I'm sorry baby, I'm sure nobody noticed."

"You don't know that," Trish said. She looked around. She felt like everyone was staring at them.

The ADHD Vampire

"You're being ridiculous," Martha said. She reached out and put her hand on Trish's arm. Trish jerked away.

"Are you serious?" Trish said. "I can't do this out here. You're drunk, or else you wouldn't be acting like this."

Trish turned and ran away from Martha. Martha watched as she ran. At first, she thought, screw it. Trish would calm down and see that she was overreacting. Surely she would end up coming back to apologize.

She spent the next hour dancing with guys and other women. She mingled, and since she was inebriated she had no problem talking to people she didn't know or had met only one or two other times.

A scream put a stop to the festivities. Next to the open field where they danced, there were a few trees and the grass was unkempt, reaching almost waist-high. A couple had disappeared into the thick grass for some privacy and stumbled upon a body. It was too dark to make out who it might be.

"Hey, anybody got a flashlight? I think somebody's hurt out here!" a man said, calling out to the assembling crowd.

"Yeah, I got one, just a sec," another said. He came running up from the cars, shining the light. Martha came up behind him. Her heart was pounding like crazy. She was having difficulty breathing. Her mind was racing. Has something happened to Trish? She had been gone for awhile; what if someone saw them dancing and attacked her for being with another woman? It was all her fault, she pushed it too far. If something happened to her she would never be able to live with herself.

The man with the flashlight reached the front of the crowd. He shined the light along the ground until it landed on the body. It was Trish. The side of her neck had been ripped away, like she had been attacked by some wild animal.

Martha saw her lover there on the ground, blood all around her from the neck wound. She screamed.

"Are you okay?" Martha heard somebody say. She saw the two old lesbians were looking at her. "You screamed, honey, are you okay?"

She had only been lost in her memories, she hadn't realized she screamed out like that.

"Oh, I'm sorry," Martha said the ladies. "I didn't mean to stare."

"It's okay, honey," the one on the bottom said. "You want to join us and make this a three-way?"

"No, thank you. I only like men," Martha said as she stood up and walked away.

6.

rew man Sanchez pushed a mop and bucket full of soapy water over to the blood and viscera in the cargo bay. He cussed under his breath.

"I'm getting sick of always having to clean up the messes," he said to himself. "I'm not the only nobody on this ship. The shit work needs to start being spread around."

He plopped the mop into the puddle of blood and pushed it around the floor. He really was a nobody on the ship, he knew it. He was lucky to get this shitty job. He owed a lot of money to some pretty tough madams. He couldn't help he was turned on by being thrown up on, and having his balls chewed on by midget celebrity look-a-likes. Sanchez just wanted to make enough money to pay off the debt he had wracked up and to get a miniature Tiffani Amber-Thesian to shove her stubby fingers up his ass.

"Damn, why are old people so disgusting?" He said as he lifted the mop up and dripped vile liquid back onto the floor. He was startled as he heard a noise coming from behind one of the crates. "It's so creepy down here. Damn, this sucks!"

He mopped faster. The blood spread out along the floor instead of coming clean. There was another noise, louder this time. Sanchez stopped mopping.

"Okay, I get it. Someone thought it would be funny to fuck with me?" he said to the shadows. "Well, haha, I can take a joke. I'm a cool guy. Now, come on out."

Sanchez leaned the mop against the bucket and stepped toward the open crate. There was another noise and Sanchez stopped.

"Come on guys, don't take this too far. We're stuck on this boat together, ya know. You don't want me pissed at you the whole time." He listened, figuring he would hear some laughing or something. He could make out a figure in the shadows and took a step back. The figure moved toward him, almost like it was gliding across the floor. Sanchez was preparing to go back and grab the mop to use as a weapon when he realized it was just an old lady.

"Hey, miss, you don't need to be down here," he said. He relaxed as she came toward him. The closer she got, the more he noticed details about her.

The front of her shirt was covered in blood.

"Hey, are you okay?" he asked. He walked to meet her. "Were you attacked down here, too? Let me help you."

As they closed in on each other, she put her arms up to catch him in an embrace. She opened her mouth, and that's when Sanchez saw her fangs.

She grabbed him before he could react and sank her teeth into his neck. She was over-excited and pulled back, ripping a chunk of meat away. He fought back and discovered that for an old lady, she was incredibly strong. He pulled himself from her grasp. The woman put her fingers up to her mouth and eagerly licked and sucked at Sanchez's blood.

The ADHD Vampire

"What the hell is wrong with you?" he asked. He held a hand tight against his neck, but the blood just poured out around his fingers. The old woman looked up at him and smiled crazily. Sanchez turned and took off as fast as he could, tripping over the mop and bucket along the way.

The lady took a step to go after him and kicked the mop as it lay on the floor. She reached down and picked it up. Sanchez chanced a look back as the crazy lady threw the mop toward him, handle first. He slipped and fell forward as the mop handle made contact, impaling him through his asshole. His body crumpled to the floor as the old woman vampire pounced on him and began to feed again.

7.

elilah smiled politely at Martha as they walked past each other in the corridor. Neither one knew they both had the same agenda that night. One of them was leaving the captain, while the other one was going to see him. Both women, however, had noticed the other talking and flirting with the captain. So as Delilah politely smiled at Martha, Martha returned her smile with one equally as polite, but they were both hiding jealous anger behind those smiles. Delilah couldn't help but feel a little smug, having just come from a pleasant evening of naughty sex with the captain. She had drank enough wine and felt nice and inebriated, to the point where she almost wanted to share her little secret with this tramp, to goad and lord it over her. But that wouldn't be lady-like, and Delilah was a lady before anything else, regardless of how much wine she drank, with the exception of behind closed doors. She wasn't exactly lady-like with the captain earlier, but that's her only exception.

Martha glanced back at Delilah and saw her stagger a bit. She covered her mouth to keep a laugh from escaping. *Stupid bitch* she thought to herself. I wonder how she would feel to know the captain personally invited me into his cabin?

She felt a little giddy with anticipation. She fully planned to fuck the shit out of the captain, to do things with him that would make prissy little Delilah blush. She fully intended to go and rub it in her face afterwards, which would be the following morning, when she'd wake up in the captain's bed.

***

The captain smiled at the sound of knocking on his door. *Ah, Martha*, he thought to himself.

"Come on in," he said as he lay back on his bed, a glass of wine in hand. His attitude completely changed when the door opened and instead of Martha, first mate Ryan stepped inside.

"Sorry to disturb you, Captain," he said.

"What the devil? What do you want this time?" the captain said as he stood up from his bed.

"Well, I wanted to tell you we have a couple of missing passengers," Ryan said. He glanced around the room, making sure he wasn't interrupting anything as he had before.

"Missing passengers?" the captain repeated.

"Yes, sir. I wouldn't have said anything if it was just one, but we have three separate people missing since dinner."

The captain stroked his beard. He sipped from his wine, then set the glass down.

"The people aboard this ship are very old, son. Before we go jumping to any conclusions, we're going to need to check every part of this ship," the captain said. "I know you can handle it, son. I'm sure the passengers will turn up."

"Aye aye, Captain," Ryan said and nodded his

head, confident he knew what do to, and left the room. He almost ran into Martha, who was standing outside the door and listening to their conversation.

"Excuse me, ma'am. I am very sorry," Ryan said.

She smiled at him. "It's okay, dear. You just startled me a little." She went to the open door of the captain's room. The captain sat on the edge of his bed, his hand stroking his beard. He was staring off into space, clearly deep in thought.

The captain had tried to sound reassuring to his first mate, but the truth was he thought the disappearances seemed strange. He hadn't noticed Martha standing there.

"Hello, Captain, my captain," she said, pulling him away from his thoughts.

"Well, come on in, my dear. Let me pour you a drink." Martha entered the cabin and shut the door behind her. She had heard everything they said about the disappearances. She knew she was going to have to do something about it. She felt it was her duty as an ex-secret agent. Martha had pledged an oath when she joined The Company, even though she retired from that lifestyle twenty years ago. When she signed on and let them install robotics into half her body, making her a cyborg, she had signed on for life.

She walked up and took the glass of wine the captain held out for her, and sat down on his lap. She would investigate what was happening on the ship, but first she was going to have a little fun with the half of her body that was still flesh and blood.

8.

Did you see that wrinkly mess the captain had with him today?" Officer of the watch Stuart Adams said as he stared out the window from the bridge. The only other person around was helmsman Kelly Grover, and he had no desire to get into this discussion with Officer Adams.

"I am so sick of looking at all these ugly old people," Adams continued. "When this tour is over, I'm going to have to transfer to a ship that actually attracts hot, young pussy."

Kelly rolled his eyes and kept looking ahead at the monitor. They were in open water now, so he didn't technically need to sit at the helm and guide the ship, but his only other option was to talk to Officer Adams, and he just sucked.

"What about you?" Adams asked, turning around to face Kelly. "I never see you chatting with any of these old broads, you more into chicks your own age? Or are you into chicks at all?"

Kelly swiveled his chair around to face the officer but didn't get a chance to respond.

"What the crap is that?" Adams said, pointing past Kelly, towards the door. "Is that smoke?"

Kelly turned to see what he was pointing at. Something was coming onto the bridge from under the door, but it wasn't smoke. There was no smell, and it wasn't thick at all. It was more like a fog, or a mist. Kelly stood up as Adams walked over to investigate, reaching out to touch it.

The mist swirled around Adams' out-stretched arm, then up his body. It acted as if it had a mind of its own. Adams' eyes went wide, then the mist formed into a man, and Horace had a hand around Adam's throat. Kelly fell backward over his chair.

Horace was full on vampire feeding mode when something flashed out of the corner of his eye. He turned his head and saw the control console of the ship. His eyes went wide and he swung around fast, Adams still in his grasp.

"What do you think you're doing?" Kelly asked. Horace was hovering over the flashing lights, indicators, and gauges with excitement. "Leave that stuff alone."

Kelly wanted to be brave, but he was scared and stayed on the floor with his chair in front of him for protection.

Horace leaned onto the console, Adams throat still grasped tightly. The vampire was completely unaware that the officer was still in his grasp. As he leaned in to check out the various lights, he smashed the struggling man's face into the controls. A buzzer sounded from behind Horace and he turned toward it, smacking Adams' face into a small panel above the console. There was a bright red strobe light attached to the buzzer.

While Horace was distracted by the strobe light and buzzer, Kelly forced himself past his fear and jumped up to the console. He needed to correct whatever Horace had done to set off the alarm.

When the ship was back on track, the alarm stopped. Kelly froze; he felt exposed just standing for whoever this crazy person was to attack. He slowly turned, and sure enough, Horace was standing there looking at him.

"Who are you, what do you want?" Kelly asked the man. He tried his best to keep the fear out of his voice.

"My name is Horace Dracul. I am here to feed off you."

"Me?" Kelly said, pointing at himself. He then pointed at Adams. "What about him?"

Horace looked down at the bloody and bruised man he still had around the neck like he was seeing him for the first time.

"Oh, yeah," Horace said. "Him too."

With ridiculous speed, Horace had Adams' neck up to his mouth and was draining the wounded man on the spot. Kelly screamed in a high-pitched tone normally associated with females. He managed to unfreeze his legs and start for the door, but Horace threw Adams at him. The weight of the lifeless man caused Kelly to slam into a wall and crumble to the floor.

Horace started toward the two bodies on the floor when he saw the large monitor above the console displaying swirling weather patterns. He turned and went to the monitor, his face inches away as the greens and blues twirled and danced before him.

Kelly carefully slid out from under Adams' body. The officer moaned when Kelly moved him. Horace turned toward the men as Kelly was standing up. The vampire started to move toward the escaping seaman

Matthew Vaughn

but his eyes didn't want to leave the magnificent console.

Every move Kelly made for the door brought Horace closer. Horace continued to struggle with the overwhelming need to look at the flashing lights and pretty colors, and the desire to drain Kelly of all his blood.

Putting his hand on the door handle, Kelly thought he was free for sure. But then something grabbed his ankle. It was Adams, looking up at him, his eyes pleading. Kelly lifted his leg to try and shake the man's grasp. He felt like it would be wrong to leave the man behind, but he was going to anyway.

The more Kelly shook his leg, the tighter Adams' grip became. Then Horace managed to pull himself away and pounced on Adams. Kelly screamed in his high-pitched, lady-like scream, but the officer still didn't let go of his leg. It didn't matter, since Kelly had lost all common sense and forgot to run instead of scream his head off. He screamed until Horace was finished with Adams and turned his attention on him.

9.

When Delilah tumbled down the stairs, she knew she was drunk. She felt silly. It was only three steps. Even though her head hurt, she still laughed, which made her pee a little bit. This was not like her. She was all about having a good time behind a closed and locked door, but to get drunk and stumble around in public? She was embarrassed. The captain was just too persuasive; his charm was overpowering.

She sat on the floor in front of the small set of steps and felt her head. There was a tender spot. When she looked at her hand, she saw blood.

Delilah tried standing up. She got dizzy and fell back onto her ass. Her tail bone caught the edge of the bottom step.

"Oh, ow!" she said. She rolled over onto her side and arched her back as she caressed her bruised tail bone.

Lying on the floor, she started to think she may be in trouble. She looked around for something to use to help her stand up. There was nothing. She closed her eyes and her head started spinning. She scolded herself for having drunk too much, something she wouldn't normally do.

When she opened her eyes, she saw a figure standing at the far corner.

"Hello, there. Could you please help me?" she asked the person. She was squinting her eyes, trying to make the person out. Her eyesight wasn't too good anymore, but she didn't feel pretty or sexy in her glasses, so she hadn't brought them when she went to visit the Captain. Something wet ran down her forehead and into her eyes. She wiped away what she could and looked at her hands. It was blood. She must have hit her head harder than she thought.

"Please help me!" she cried out. When she looked to the corner where the mysterious figure had been, it was gone.

"Why, I can't believe this! What a . . . a piece of crap!" she said. She didn't care about being lady-like now. More blood ran down her forehead and into her eyes. She wiped at her eyes again and started to feel woozy. Delilah stopped and took a couple good, deep breaths. She decided, right then and there, she wasn't going to give up. She was determined not to die lying on the floor like some broken old lady.

She was going to climb the steps. She flipped over onto her belly and saw a pair of boots directly in front of her face, between her and the steps.

"You look like you could use some help," a man said to her.

Delilah looked up and saw Horace looking down at her. He opened his mouth and bared his fangs. That was the last thing she saw before she passed out.

***

When Delilah opened her eyes, the world around her was blurry. Her head hurt. She reached a hand up to the sore spot and was relieved that it wasn't bleeding anymore. Her hair was sticky with dried blood. She put her hand down to try and lift herself up and realized she was lying on a soft bed.

The world was starting to come into focus, as much as it could without her glasses. She looked over to her right and saw a set of ugly, sagging tits. Startled, she scooted back and bumped into something. She turned to look behind her and saw another set of sagging tits, these on the wrinkled body of an old woman she didn't recognize. She was completely naked, except for a tube running around her face and under her nose. She turned back to the first pair of breasts and saw an old wrinkly face she recognized.

"Estelle? What's going on here, why are you naked?" Delilah asked.

"Oh, Delilah, we were just getting ready to have a little fun with you," Estelle said to her. The old woman behind her laughed.

Delilah looked away from Estelle, who she thought was her friend, to the other lady.

"Yes, just lay back now, deary. It will be over before you know it," Rachelle, the old lady Delilah didn't recognize, said. She opened her mouth and hissed at Delilah, fangs sharp and prominent.

Delilah screamed and covered her face. Estelle grabbed her right arm and Rachelle grabbed her left. They pulled Delilah's arms out away from her body. She struggled, but the vampires were too strong. They forced her back down onto the bed. Each one bit into the wrist they were holding. Delilah stopped thrashing and relaxed as they drained her of her blood. Estelle lifted her head up away from Delilah's arm. Blood ran down the sides of her mouth as she let out a pleasure-filled moan. She went back down to bite Delilah's arm again but she couldn't break through the flesh. She tried again and again before finally lifting her head up. She immediately saw her problem; her dentures had stayed stuck in Delilah's arm when she lifted her head the first time. She lowered her head again, this time taking the dentures back into her mouth to enjoy more delicious blood.

Delilah's eyes were heavy. They fluttered and she was slowly giving up on trying to keep them open. Before she let go completely, she saw a man standing at the foot of the bed. Horace smiled at her, and then her eyes closed.

10.

Horace felt like a vampire king. For the first time in his life, he felt powerful and important. He sat in a nice, comfortable chair in one of the passenger cabins. He had an old, frail man, seventy-seven year old Maxwell, pinned across his lap. Maxwell was unconscious, but still alive. He had let his bladder go when Horace appeared out of nowhere, but the old man had just recently changed his adult diaper before he was attacked, so the piss was well contained.

It wasn't the strong grip of Horace, or the snarling and baring of his teeth that caused the old man to pass out. It was when Horace pulled the old man across his lap and he saw the three women half covered in blood. They had sharp teeth and were anxious to sink them into him. It was all too much for Maxwell. His world faded to black.

The three ladies all crowded around Horace's feet, waiting for him to rip open the old geezer in his lap. To him, they felt like his disciples, worshiping at his feet, waiting with bated breath for him to drain Maxwell into them.

"My lovelies," he said. "My beautiful brides. I have

created you three to stay with me forever. We are forever bonded with my blood that now flows through your veins."

"Yes, my master," Rachelle said. Estelle and Delilah murmured their agreement. They writhed at his feet, hungry with anticipation.

"My brother had three brides at one time," Horace said. "Just like with everything else, he used them to taunt me and pick on me. Dracula, he was such a dick. Everybody thinks he was so special, while I was just a nobody."

Horace put his hand on the back of Maxwell's neck. The three vampire women at his feet became excited, they could barely contain themselves. Their eyes grew wide, expecting him to slice through the pink flesh and allow them to feed, but he did no such thing.

"The four of us will show them, though. This boat will be just the beginning. I want to bring fear to the humans. I want them to treat me as their king." Horace moved his hand away from the old man's neck. The three women watched the hand move away in disappointment. "No more will I be living in the shadow of my brother. I will make my own place in this world. Legends will be written about me, Horace Dracul, and everyone will forget all about Vlad. My father, may he rot in Hell, will see what his second son is capable of. The son he called stupid and weak, frail like a woman."

Estelle, Rachelle, and Delilah all looked at each other. They shrugged in confusion. They didn't want to interrupt their master, but he had really gone off subject.

"They mocked my manhood. They took any woman from me that I showed the smallest amount of interest in. My father forced me to sleep out with the dogs, and they treated me better than my own family did!" Horace grew angrier as he recounted childhood memories. "What do you think now, father? What do you think about the son you accused of wanting to lay down with another man? The son you said was born without his manhood and instead came to sire children?"

"Um, master?" Delilah said, finally finding the courage to address his inability to focus on the situation at hand. Horace looked down at her like he had forgotten she was there. "Sorry my lord, but the human is waking up."

Horace looked at the old man in his lap.

"Uh, yeah. We probably need to dispose of him," Horace said. He took the sharp nail of his pinky finger and ran it across the old man's neck. A thin, red line appeared underneath the man's chin. Horace pulled the man's head backwards, and as the red line opened, his blood began to pour out. The three female vamps eagerly fought to lap up the crimson liquid. Horace watched his three brides dine, but part of his mind was still lingering on the past.

***

First Mate Ryan had every intention of following his captain's order. The problem was the majority of the passengers aboard the ship were asleep in their cabins. It was the middle of the night, and since most of the passengers were old, they were in bed by eight o'clock or so. He could recruit a couple of crewmembers to search various areas of the ship, but he wasn't about to go door to door and check every passenger. He was sure the complaints that corporate would receive would get him fired.

As he turned the corner and started down the corridor to the passenger's cabins, he was almost knocked off his feet by the smell of shit. He used his hand to cover his nose and mouth, but it was too late. He could taste it. Maybe it had coated his hand with the smell of diarrhea, or it was clinging to his nose hairs. Whatever the case, he could not stop gagging as he walked.

He came to a door that was partially open and noticed the smell of feces was pretty potent there. He didn't really want to be anywhere near it, but he felt it was his duty to investigate.

Hesitantly, he pushed the door open and peered inside. Something rose up into his throat and he gagged again, trying to choke it back down. So much for trying to be quiet, he thought.

Ryan felt along the wall next to the door for the light switch. He flipped it on and saw the wet, nasty shit that was making the room smell bad. It looked like one of the passengers made the middle of their cabin a toilet. What was even more disturbing was the amount of blood mixed in it.

Ryan looked around the small room and saw no sign of its occupant. *Somewhere there is an old man or woman with something seriously wrong*, he thought to himself.

Ryan walked out of the room and back into the corridor. For the first time, he noticed a trail of blood leading away from the cabin. He decided to follow it and see where it would lead.

11.

orace Dracul stood near the bar, mesmerized by the TV. He decided he would feast on the remaining occupants of the ship, and had been making his way past the lounge, when the flickering of the television grabbed his attention and he stopped. He didn't know what he was watching. It was clearly a drama, a police drama by the looks of it, but Horace's lack of attention didn't allow him to focus on programs for very long, let alone multiple episodes week after week.

Already bored with the TV, Horace walked behind the bar. He liked the shiny silver handles on the beer taps. He pulled them one at a time and watched as one poured a golden colored liquid. The next was a dark brown. One was a color somewhere between the two, and the last was the darkest of all, almost black. He pulled the handle on the darkest one and watched it pour out, filling the pan underneath, before swirling down the drain.

"Hey, now!" a voice from behind Horace said. "What do you think you're doing?"

It was then that Horace remembered what he was planning on doing before coming into the lounge. He turned and saw a short, stocky man with an apron.

"Who the hell are you?" the man asked. "You don't look like a passenger."

"I am Horace Dracul."

"What the fuck kinda name is that? Like Dracula or something?" the man asked. Horace smirked.

"The Dracula you are referring to is my older brother, Vlad," Horace said as he walked towards the man.

"I ain't never heard any such nonsense! Dracula having a goofy little brother?" The man untied his apron and threw it on the counter. "Listen boy, I don't know if you're a stow-away or what, but I'm taking you to the captain."

Horace started thinking about his older brother and about how he used to pick on him. He had always had problems with paying attention and being able to keep still, but Vlad just bullied him and teased him for not being smart. Horace had tried as hard as he could to live up to the family name. Even as an undead vampire, he tried to create a menacing name for himself. Everything was so much harder for Horace.

He then realized the short man was pulling on him, trying to drag him out of the lounge.

"Your efforts are worthless, little man," Horace said. He slipped easily out of the man's grip.

"I just told you I'm a retired Navy Seal, didn't you hear me?" the old man asked as he placed himself in a fighting stance. "You are coming with me, even if I have to make you!"

The man lunged for Horace, and the vampire reached a hand out and grabbed the man by the throat. He effortlessly lifted the man into the air.

The ADHD Vampire

"No, little man. I am a Dracul, I go only where I want to go." Horace tossed the small man into the shelf behind the bar. The shelf was demolished and liquor bottles fell to the floor and shattered. Horace wasn't very thirsty for blood at the moment, so he had a hard time staying focused on what he was doing. He turned away from the bar and made for the exit.

"Hey, fucker," came a shaky voice from behind him. He turned to see the short old man stepping out from behind the bar. He had multiple cuts on his face, and blood was all over his clothing. The smell of it made Horace's appetite return.

"I'm an ex-Navy Seal for the U. S. of gat-damn A." the man said. "It's gonna take more than that to keep me down."

Horace had the man's head in his hands and his teeth in his throat before the ex-Navy Seal even knew what was happening.

12.

ucinda tossed and turned in the bed. George lay next to her, snoring. She shoved him a couple good times; she had heard people stopped snoring when they rolled over, but he wouldn't budge.

They had met earlier in the day. They each had brought along a date and when the four of them met, they decided to try a little swinging. Why she agreed to let George sleep over in her room, she didn't know. She was a light sleeper anyway, but this was ridiculous. She should have insisted on a *wham-bam-thank-you-ma'am,* and then got on with a good night's rest.

Lucinda decided maybe a late night stroll around the ship would do her some good. Climbing out of the bed was never an easy task for the eighty-four year old, but she remained surprised at how deeply George could sleep. He never moved or woke once. She looked down and realized that she had fallen asleep naked. She was disgusted by her old and wrinkled body. She hated her sagging tits and belly fat, but at her age there wasn't anything that could be done about it. She dressed in her pajamas and wrapped a robe around her body.

The ADHD Vampire

As she opened the door that would take her out to the hallway, Lucinda noticed a strange smell. It smelled as if somebody had shit themselves nearby her cabin. It reminded her that she didn't put on an adult diaper. She didn't always have a problem with her bowels, but there had been a couple instances, and that was enough for her to take the necessary precautions. She wore a diaper anytime she would be away from home, or at a new place where she might not know exactly where the toilet was.

Turning to go back inside, she heard a noise and looked down the hallway. There was a figure, but in the poor lighting she couldn't make out who it was. It was heading her direction and the closer it got she could tell it was a woman. Then she could see the blood on her clothing and thought she was hurt.

Lucinda stepped out into the hallway, forgetting all about her diaper problems and George and his snoring.

"Hello? Are you okay, you look hurt," she said as she approached the woman. The woman, Estelle, did not answer. As she came closer, she recognized the woman from around the ship, but she didn't know her name.

"What happened to you? Come here, let me help you," Lucinda said. Estelle still didn't answer, but as she got closer, she opened her mouth to reveal a set of fangs. Lucinda let out a piercing scream and the woman lunged at her.

First Mate Ryan came running around the corner. He was just in time to see Estelle as she began feasting violently on Lucinda. Ryan made a move to try and help the woman being attacked when an old man stepped out of the room in front of him and they collided. Both men tumbled over each other in a tangle of limbs.

"My hip!" the old man shouted. Ryan looked up to see what was happening with the lady being attacked, but doors were opening all along the hallway. Old people in pajamas, night gowns, and some half-naked, were pouring into the hallway.

"What the hell is going on out here?" said one old man displaying a full upper body tattoo.

"Somebody screaming and yelling?" a woman in skimpy red lingerie near him asked.

Another old lady in a robe let out a scream when she saw Lucinda lying on the ground, blood pooled around her neck. Then she turned and saw Estelle standing next to Lucinda's body. She had blood covering her mouth and chin, running down the front of her, and staining her shirt. The old lady let out another loud, piercing scream. Estelle punched the screaming old lady so hard her head ripped off her neck and went flying behind her. The head hit another old man standing in nothing but stained tighty-whities. The wet thud on his back wasn't enough to knock him over, he just turned to see what had hit him. When he saw the severed head staring back up at him, he clutched his chest in pain and fell over dead.

From there, the hallway erupted in chaos. The old people nearest Estelle tried to get away from her as she grabbed a nearby old lady. She sunk her teeth into the screaming lady as geriatrics pushed each other down, trying to keep from being her next meal.

Some of the people in the hallway were smart enough to just go back into their rooms, but not many. One old man, seventy-two year old Earl, who was dressed in a long red robe, got confused with all the chaos around him. Without thinking, he reached out and grabbed the nearest person to him and attacked them.

Sixty-five year old Grace was frightened enough by what had been taking place, since she was awoken by a scream in the middle of night, but when the older gentlemen next to her turned and grabbed her by her nightgown, she thought for sure she would soil herself.

Earl pulled Grace close to his wrinkled face, so close she could smell the polident he used on his dentures.

"You're not taking me alive, you Jap bastard!" he screamed. He then leaned in and bit her left ear off.

Grace screamed and her seventy-six year old husband, Fred, who had also seen action in Vietnam, turned to see her being held by the crazed Earl. Grace's blood was spraying onto nearby people while Earl chewed on her ear. His dentures cracked on the diamond earring Grace always wore.

Fred dropped his walker to the floor and tackled the blood-covered Earl. Earl let go of Grace when Fred made impact, and as they tumbled, his robe fell open, revealing the bright red lingerie he wore underneath.

Grace continued to scream as First Mate Ryan reached her. He found a discarded woman's silk robe wadded up on the floor.

"Here, press this against your head," he told Grace. He pushed the bundle of cloth to her head and she freaked out again.

"It's okay, I'm trying to help you," he said to her. He then realized that she was looking past him. He turned and saw Estelle covered in blood, baring her fangs at them.

Estelle reached out and grabbed First Mate Ryan and tore into his neck. Grace screamed until she was hoarse and couldn't scream anymore, but she kept trying. Her mouth was wide open when Ryan's blood sprayed her down.

The crowd of elderly passengers was being whittled down. Rachelle was on one end of the hallway tearing into people who had fallen, or were too frightened to move. The ones who did move ran right into Estelle. A few of them made it around the vampires, but not many.

At this time, Horace showed up to enjoy all the death and destruction.

13.

The captain propped himself up on one arm to watch Martha's ass as she walked across his cabin to the restroom. He was amazed at how fit she was for a woman of her age. She had her wrinkles, her sagging ass and tits, but they weren't to the extent of the usual old women he banged. This one took care of herself, even in her eighties. And who could even tell she was that age? The captain would have guessed late fifties, mid-sixties at the most. But eighty-four? It was unbelievable. He wanted another go around with this freaky momma. He opened up the drawer on the table next to his bed to pull out his bottle of Viagra, but was distracted when he heard a commotion out in the hallway.

The captain climbed out of bed and grabbed a robe off a nearby chair. Martha came out of the bathroom and the captain was disappointed to see her in her bra and panties.

"Oh, are you in a rush?" he asked her. As she walked over in her skimpy underwear, he felt his penis start to grow. *Might not need that Viagra after all*, he thought.

Martha walked up to the captain, gently grabbed his head, and kissed him passionately on the lips.

"I've had a wonderful time. You are a very naughty boy," she said to him, her lips spread into a smile. "But there is something I need to do. When I'm done, I will gladly come back."

The captain opened his mouth to speak, but was interrupted by a scream out in the hallway.

"What the hell?" they both said. The captain went to the door as Martha quickly pulled on her clothing.

The captain was not prepared for what he saw in the hallway. He had been a captain for thirty years, half of that time on a cruise ship just like this. In all that time, he had never had to deal with a full-scale panic, riot, or whatever it was he was witnessing.

He watched passengers and crew members as they ran down the hallway. Some were bloody, some were screaming. It was clear they were all afraid of something.

"What is all that?" Martha asked. She sat on the edge of the bed, tying her shoes. The captain, still standing in the doorway, turned to tell her what he saw. He didn't get a word out before Estelle grabbed him from behind.

Martha watched as the old lady vampire feasted on the captain. Like the flip of a switch, her training and instincts kicked in. She jumped up from the bed and took off running toward the two figures in the doorway.

Assuming that the captain was already well on his way to death, she flipped into the air and planted both her feet into his chest. Her speed and strength pushed both the captain and his attacker out of the doorway and across the hall. The vampire separated from its meal on impact, and it was pissed. Estelle bared her teeth at Martha and let out a terrifying screech. It didn't faze the ex-secret agent. She simply moved into a fighting stance and waited for the blood sucker to make a move.

Estelle leaped at Martha, who stood her ground and waited for the vampire to get as close as possible. At the precise moment, she grabbed Estelle's arms and flipped her over her head. She slammed her onto the floor. Martha didn't let go of Estelle, but instead planted her cyborg leg onto the vamp's chest and yanked back, ripping Estelle's arms from their sockets. Estelle screamed and hissed at Martha, then bucked her chest and threw the woman off.

Martha did a back flip into the air and landed on her feet. She was still holding Estelle's arms. Estelle jumped up onto her feet and screamed at Martha before charging her.

The ex-spy held her ground and waited. When Estelle was within reach, she clocked her with her own fists, first the right and then the left. The vampires severed left arm snapped in two as Estelle flew back.

What the hell is she? Martha asked herself. But deep down she knew and just didn't want to believe it. A vampire. Regardless of whether it was true or not, Martha knew she needed to put the creature down.

She got her chance when Estelle bared her fangs and charged Martha again. This time, the cyborg flipped over Estelle, landed behind her, and grabbed the sides of her head with both hands. Without much effort, she twisted Estelle's head straight off her neck. She tossed the severed head aside as the old lady vampire's body collapsed to the floor.

Matthew Vaughn

Though Martha didn't believe in vampires, it was obvious this crazy person wasn't human. Nobody that has their arms ripped off keeps getting up, trying to kill you. So, not wanting to take any chances, Martha went back into the captain's cabin. Along the left wall sat an old wooden desk and chair. She walked over, picked up the chair, and smashed it on the ground. She chose a nice spike-shaped piece of wood and took it out into the hallway.

Martha looked down at the headless body and felt a little silly. But then she thought she saw it twitch so she slammed the piece of broken chair into its chest. There wasn't any reason to take chances.

The ex-spy walked down the corridor in the direction the passengers and crew had been running. There were a lot of bodies strewn about; blood was on everything. She saw no movement. Everybody was dead. The bodies littered about reminded her of Trish, as her neck was ripped open in a similar manner to a lot of these bodies. Could whatever have killed Trish all those years ago be related to this crazy person? Could there very well be vampires in the world after all?

She heard a scream coming from the direction she was headed. It appeared to be coming from outside on the deck. Martha picked up the pace and went to investigate.

14.

Seventy-nine year old Redford had to come up for air. He lifted his head up, and the dildo strapped to his forehead bent down and touched his nose as it slid out of the grey haired vagina in front of his face. When it exited the glistening hole it made a 'plop' sound and bounced above his eyes. A queef followed the plastic shlong just as Redford took in a deep breath.

The room smelled like sweat, Bengay, diapers, and ass. Redford inhaled again and choked up on a giggle. Someone had their false teeth out and was gumming on his ball sack. Then he felt his ass cheeks spread apart as someone started licking his asshole. Who knew a wet tongue could bring so much relief to an inflamed hemorrhoid?

Redford glanced around at the sea of flabby, sun-spotted skin. They were like one giant organism; you couldn't tell where one person's sagging skin ended and another's wrinkly ass began. There was no telling how many bodies were intertwined in this orgy.

He looked down at the grey bush in front of him and spit on the soft pink opening. Just as he started to lower his head to insert the dildo, the door to the cabin flung open.

An old woman moaned out in pleasure as Redford pushed the soft plastic dick in place. He then shoved his face into the wrinkly old asshole below it. He, along with everyone else in the room, was unaware of the two old lady vampires that had just entered the room.

Delilah went to the right after walking through the doorway, while Rachelle went left, pulling her oxygen tank behind her. They circled around the sea of sweaty, flabby flesh. The vampire's eyes were wide with excitement; they practically drooled on themselves.

Rachelle reached down and grabbed an erect penis that was nearby. She squeezed it pretty hard and the man the dick was attached to moaned loudly. She stroked it a couple times. Leaning over, Rachelle put her mouth around it. The entire shaft disappeared inside and she closed her lips around it. She pulled back, her teeth gently dragging across the skin until they reached the bottom of the swollen head. The vampire brought her teeth together and bit off the head of the man's cock. He screamed out so high-pitched that everyone in the room thought it was a woman reaching orgasm. Blood sprayed out of the damaged organ and Rachelle took it in the face like the money shot in a porno.

Sixty-seven year old Janice, with her breasts sagging so bad they hung under each armpit, felt the warm blood land on her face. She eagerly licked it and rubbed at it with her hands, then rubbed those hands around on her body. Janice never opened her eyes to see it wasn't sperm.

The ADHD Vampire

Rachelle reached down and grabbed a handful of hair. She pulled up seventy-eight year old Rebekah, who had a bouncing strap on around her waist and a vibrator in each hand. Rebekah screamed when she turned her head and saw the fangs of the vampire. Rachelle put both hands around the woman's throat and squeezed until her head popped off. She held the severed head in the air and let the blood pour down onto her.

Seventy-one year old Stanley, who was just having his asshole reamed by one of the vibrators Rebekah was holding, turned to see why she had stopped. When he saw the vampire holding the severed head, he didn't even have a chance to scream. His chest exploded in pain, first from a heart attack, but then the pain changed when Delilah shoved her hand into his chest and pulled out the arresting heart.

At this point, the orgy stopped. Sweaty old people pulled objects from various orifices and screamed in panic. The vampires tore into the naked geriatrics like children at their gifts on Christmas morning.

The massacre didn't take more than a few minutes. In the end, there was only a bloody pile of body parts, dildos, and anal beads. The two vampires left the room in search of their next prey.

15.

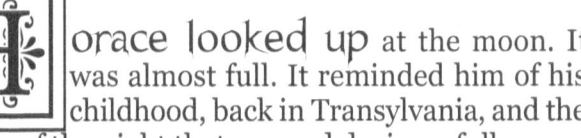orace looked up at the moon. It was almost full. It reminded him of his childhood, back in Transylvania, and the children of the night that roamed during a full moon, the blood moon, as it was called.

Something moved in Horace's hands, pulling him from his distant thoughts. He looked down and saw the old man he was holding against the floor. He had his right hand on the man's head, shoving it onto the deck of the boat. He had the old man's arm bent behind his back at an angle it was not meant to be twisted in. It took Horace a second to remember what he had been doing before the sight of the moon had distracted him.

Horace stood and yanked the frail man up off the ground in the process. His dinner dangled in the air for just a second before Horace sunk his teeth into its neck. The man screamed out, until Horace tore a huge chunk away, rendering him silent. He held the limp body up and let the blood pour into his mouth. Once he got his fill, he easily tossed the dying body aside. It hit the railing and flipped over, into the deep, dark ocean water.

The ADHD Vampire

Horace looked on at the destruction being wrought before his eyes. His two remaining brides were having their way with some of the remaining crew and passengers. They let the humans try to run as they screamed for their lives and then they would pounce on them like wild beasts out on the hunt. The vampires ripped limbs from bodies and tore open flesh. Everything was covered in blood.

Horace felt the death of his third bride, and it made him sad she wasn't here with them. He was sure she would have enjoyed this, even though they didn't have a chance to spend a lot of time together. There was a deep connection between him and his brides. The loss of his bride was something he would never forget.

Horace was pulled from his thoughts by a commotion, and he never thought about his fallen bride again. He stood from his makeshift throne, the lifeguard's chair at the pool, and floated down to the deck of the ship. His brides had disappeared. He heard something coming from around the corner and decided to investigate. Just before he rounded the corner, Horace heard an agonizing scream; he knew it was from one of his brides. He turned the corner and saw an old lady holding Rachelle by her throat, lifting her body up into the air, the oxygen tank dangling by the tubes around her throat. In the woman's other hand was Rachelle's heart. Delilah was on the ground in front of them. She had been the source of the screaming, distraught over her sister's death.

Martha looked up from the heart in her hand, dripping blood on the deck of the ship, to the man who had just appeared. He had a commanding presence, it made her think that he was the leader, that he was the one behind this. She squeezed with her bionic strength and the heart exploded into chunks, splattering her, the wall, and Delilah.

"Oh, you bitch!" Delilah hissed at her. She licked her dead partner's blood off her lips. "You will pay for her death!"

Martha was worried that destroying the heart would not be enough to stop the vampire. As much as she did not want to believe it, she knew that's what she was dealing with now. She took Rachelle's body in her right arm and squeezed tight as she separated her head from her shoulders. Delilah hissed again and charged toward Martha. Martha tossed the two parts of the dead vampire and prepared for another fight by placing herself in an impenetrable defensive stance.

Horace Dracul watched his remaining bride as she launched herself into the air at her opponent, who jumped into Delilah's path.

This woman, Horace thought, *would make a wonderful vampire. I must turn her.*

He felt like there was something very important he needed to do, but he couldn't remember what it was. He could not take his eyes from one of the final battles of the night. He was anxious to see the outcome.

16.

elilah's fingers ended in razor sharp claws, which Martha dodged by moving left, then right, and left again. Delilah was fast. She slashed at Martha with precision and ferocity. It didn't matter though. Martha had learned more fighting styles and techniques than she could remember. But she didn't need to remember them, they were programmed into her, and once a battle started, she could sit back and allow her programming to take over. She dodged back and forth until she saw that perfect moment. Delilah thrust her arm out. Martha moved, but could feel the air as the vampire's claws came within millimeters of ripping off her skin.

Martha twisted her body toward the vampire and threw her fist up, connecting with Delilah's extended elbow. The arm bent in the opposite direction it was meant to. Delilah screamed as Martha grabbed her wrist and ripped her arm off from the elbow down.

As blood sprayed from her left arm stump, Delilah brought her right claws up to Martha's face. She almost stabbed her straight on, but missed. There was a time when Martha was the best damn cyborg spy the government had on its payroll. She may be older, but she still had those skills.

Just as the tips of Delilah's claws reached a hair in front of her face, Martha snatched three of the fingers in her mouth and ripped them off the vampire's hand. Then, purely on instinct, she grabbed Delilah by the chin. With her left hand, she punched Delilah in the chest. It sent the woman flying across the deck, her jaw still firmly grasped in Martha's right hand.

Tossing the useless jaw aside, Martha jumped into the air and landed astride the fallen vampire. Delilah made gurgling sounds through all the blood pooled up in her shredded mouth. Martha looked her in the eyes as she punched her fist into the wounded creature's chest and ripped her heart out. Their eyes were still locked as Martha gave the organ a good squeeze and bits of muscle and blood splattered everywhere.

Martha tossed the dead heart behind her and looked up to where she had seen a man standing during the fight. Whoever he was he wasn't there anymore. Martha knew he had to be the mastermind behind this, she had been around enough diabolical madmen to know one when she'd seen them. She would find him, and she would end this.

17.

It took Martha a while to find the villain she knew was behind all of this. She checked over the whole ship, stepping over bodies and puddles of blood. The vampires had slaughtered the entire ship and left a gory scene in their wake. Martha made her way down to the cargo hold, where she finally came face to face with the man. He stood at the foot of a long, flat crate. It was unopened, with the word *fragile* written in bold black letters down the side. It was identical to the opened crate next to it, the one that had originally housed him.

Upon hearing her footsteps, Horace acknowledged her presence.

"Perhaps I should be disappointed about you defeating my brides. I am saddened by their deaths, this is true." He turned and looked at her. She could feel his gaze from across the room. "But you are a very remarkable woman, and you will make a very lovely bride."

"You can think that all you want, but it isn't going to happen," Martha said. But at the same time, she could feel his pull, and as much as she tried, it was becoming more and more difficult to fight.

"I am surprised you can resist me at all, you are very strong willed," Horace said. He stepped toward her, slowly. The closer he got, the harder it was for her to resist. "It does not matter. You cannot resist me for long."

"I don't know who you are, exactly, but I know that you are evil," Martha said. She began to break out in a full body sweat. She wanted to retreat, to just back away from him, but she could not. "You may not be the same one who killed the love of my life, but I know one of your kind did. I am going to do whatever it takes to stop you. Your life will end right here and now. I'm doing this for Trish!"

She reached up and put one hand on her chin and the other on the back of her head. Without the slightest hesitation, she twisted her head until there was an extremely loud crack. She broke her own neck. Her body fell to the floor. Horace stopped and stared at the lifeless corpse before him.

"That is something I can say I have never seen." He started to turn away from Martha's crumpled form when he saw a little red flashing light on her chest, beneath her shirt. Horace always had an attraction to lights and shiny things. He couldn't help himself and walked over to her. He stepped into the urine that was spreading out from under her, but he didn't notice. He bent down to get a good look, and that's when her eyes opened. She launched into the air and connected an uppercut to his jaw.

Horace was knocked back by the blow, stunned by her sudden awakening. He landed upside-down and clung to the ceiling of the cargo hold. He bared his teeth and hissed at her.

Martha looked up at Horace with the cold, dead

stare of her robot eyes. She was built with a failsafe. In a situation where she could be compromised, she could kill the human part of herself and the machine portion would take over and finish the job. She knew that Horace was strong and eventually would overpower her with his hypnotic gaze, so she activated the failsafe, becoming the ultimate killing machine.

Horace would never know this, though. He dropped down to her and she leapt to meet him in mid-air. Martha threw a punch as Horace dodged to the left. Her fist grazed his cheek. At the same time, Horace threw out a punch and Martha dodged left as his claws scraped the flesh off her neck. The human portion of her was dead and didn't feel any pain, so the scratch was nothing to her.

"As you can see, I'm not like my brides. They were only vampire for merely hours. I have been a vampire for centuries!" Horace's physical form disappeared into a cloud of smoke. The smoke engulfed Martha, who was switching between different optic modes, searching for her target.

Horace left his smoke form and returned to flesh behind her. He grabbed her head and wrapped his arm around her chest. Baring his teeth, he moved in to bite her neck. Martha threw her head back against his face and shattered two of his teeth.

Horace staggered backward in surprise. Martha took advantage of the situation and quickly spun around and kicked the vampire dead in his face. Horace flew backward, but managed to flip around in mid-air and land on his feet. He looked at Martha. His facial features had changed. His cheekbones protruded out and his eye sockets became more defined. He was pissed. Still hunched on the ground, but on his hands and feet, he crawled toward her, fast.

Martha crouched down into a linebacker's stance and launched herself at him. Horace flipped around at the last second, his back to the ground, and sliced her mid-section open.

Entrails and gore spilled out, but it didn't faze her. She managed to grab his ankles and flipped herself over, taking him with her. They did a two-person summersault that ended with Martha slamming Horace face first onto the floor. He rolled over and she stood above him.

The scent of her blood pouring out of the gaping wound in her abdomen was intoxicating to him. It was bright red, slick and shiny. He could not take his eyes off of it.

That is, until Martha ran her hand into his chest.

Horace stared up at her with a look of disbelief. She kept her hand in his chest, her index and middle fingers piercing his heart, until his body fell away into dust.

Martha stood up, and having completed her final mission, the computer in her brain switched off. Her dead, lifeless body crumbled to the ground.

18

Martinez looked down at his vomit, splashed on the floor between his boots. There were chunks of something, but at the moment he could not remember what he had eaten that day.

"Hey, Martinez? You gonna be okay?" he heard Attaway ask. He knew he was never going to live this down.

"Yeah, I'm fine, just caught me off guard is all," Martinez said.

"Then quit being a pussy and let's check some of the other rooms," Attaway said.

Martinez reached for the door handle to pull it closed. He kept his head down so he couldn't see the pile of dead bodies in the middle of the room. It was like nothing he had ever seen before. There was so much blood, and what looked like chunks of meat. Some of the body parts looked like they had been ripped off, and he was positive he saw a dildo, too. *What the fuck happened here?* he thought.

The U.S.S. Exciter had been found drifting along by a European fishing vessel. Any attempts at hailing the crew came up empty. The Coast Guard sent a small crew consisting of Martinez, Attaway, and four more teams of two to investigate. The boat stank of spoiled food, shit, and something else he didn't recognize. Martinez knew now the smell was death.

"Yeah, same here. Nothing but dead bodies and a big fucking mess up here, too," Attaway said into his radio. "It's like a massacre happened here or something. Do what? You found two open crates filled with dirt?"

"What the fuck is going on here Attaway?" Martinez said. He heard the radio through his headset, too. *Two identical open crates in the cargo hold?* he thought to himself.

"I don't know," Attaway said. "But the lab boys are going to have their work cut out for them, trying to piece this one together. Come on, let's finish checking this floor so we can secure the ship and get it towed in."

Martinez nodded and they walked to the next room.

Further down in the lower levels of the ship, Holloway and Jeters shined their flashlights into the crates filled with dirt.

"It doesn't make sense, what was in these things?" Jeters said. He reached a gloved hand down and pushed some of the dirt around.

"I don't know man, I don't think I would be touching any of it though," Holloway said. "Let the lab boys check it out first."

"It's just dirt, don't be stupid. It's not like it came to life and shoved that mop handle up that dead dude's ass over there. You read too many funny books and scary stories." Jeters stopped and shined his light at the ceiling. "Did you hear that?"

The ADHD Vampire

"Hear what?" Holloway asked. He shined his flashlight up to the ceiling also, the bean catching two, small gleaming objects. "What is that?"

Holloway walked toward whatever sat hidden up in the ceiling. He kept his flashlight beam trained in the area, the object still obscured by shadows and ceiling supports.

"What are you doing?" Jeters said. He looked up, trying to see what Holloway was looking at. What was up in the ceiling came down toward Holloway, who let out a scream. It was a black bat. The man ducked as the thing came toward him—he was sure it was going to attack his head. His flashlight clanked on the floor as he covered his head with his hands. Instead, the bat flew past him and attacked a key ring that lay on the floor near Sanchez's dead body.

"Holy shit! Did you see that?" Holloway said.

"Yeah, I saw you almost piss your pants!" Jeters laughed.

"Screw you dude, that was scary," Holloway said. He picked up his flashlight and checked to see if it still worked. He shined the light at Jeters. "Come on, this level is clear, let's move on."

Acknowledgements

Thanks to William Pauley III for helping me to shape this thing. His work in the initial editing was invaluable. Thanks to Pat and Vincenzo for digging this story and wanting to publish it, and especially Vincenzo for all the hard work he put into getting to this point. Most importantly, thank you to my wonderful wife, Krystal, for supporting me while I spent so much of my sparse free time working on this, you're the best!

About The Author

Matthew Vaughn lives in Shelbyville, Kentucky. He is the father of three little girls and a little boy, yet he and his wife are just big kids too. By day he maintains machines and robots, but, by night he is a writer of bizarro fiction. You can keep up with his work at http://mcvaughn.wordpress.com/ or at
https://www.facebook.com/matthew.vaughn.12532

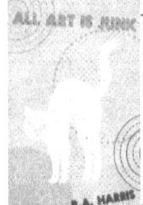

All Art is Junk by R. A. Harris

Lana Rivers, a girl with paintbrush hair, is missing and it's up to Lancelot, her cyborg knight, and his bionic conjoined twin, Cilia, to find her before her evil father, a disrespected artist turned mad-scientist, performs a terrible experiment on her.

Cherub by David C. Hayes

Cherub wasn't like the other boys—too slow, too rough—but he didn't deserve what that hospital did to him, and now he will make them pay.

Skinners by Adam Millard

Los Angeles, the City of Angels. At least, that's what the brochure says. What it fails to mention is the earthquakes. Oh, and the flesh-eating creatures lying dormant beneath the concrete, waiting for the chance to surface once again. Their wait is over . . .

The After-Life Story of Pork Knuckles Malone
by MP Johnson

What's a farm boy to do when his pet pig becomes an evil, decaying hunk of ham with slime-spewing psychic powers?

A Lightbulb's Lament by Grant Wamack

A gentleman with a lightbulb for head wakes up in a world full of darkness, hooks up with a beautiful ex-prostitute, and an old man who can heal people; he travels down south to find the mysterious Creator.

The Horror Show by Vincenzo Bilof

A poetry novel—a narcoleptic, amnesiac Nobel Prize-winning poet becomes the subject of an experiment to cure madness.

Gravity Comics Massacre
by Vincenzo Bilof

An absolutely shitty novella involving comic books, aliens, a serial killer, teenagers in an abandoned town, horror-trope dream sequences, and an ending you're going to hate.

Glue by Scott Lange

Sticky bowels and sticky situations.

Ascent by Matthew Bialer

Is the 8 foot tall creature haunting a small town in Iowa in the fall of the year 1903 the product of a hoax and collective imagination or was it one of the first documented paranormal event in America? This epic poem grapples with these questions.

Fecal Terror by David Bernstein

A killer turd is on the loose!

The Fairy Princess of Trains
by Christopher Boyle

Danny's mediocre life turns upside-down when his couch starts whispering to him. Then he's charged with a supernatural mission: Rescue the Fairy Princess of Trains.

Terence, Mephisto & Viscera Eyes
by Chris Kelso

9 new science fiction stories from Chris Kelso

Bizarro Bizarro: An Anthology

The finest bizarro short stories from 2013.

Necrosaurus Rex by Nicolas Day

Necrosaurus Rex tells the tale of Martin, a simple janitor, who takes an unfortunate trip through time, becomes a violent mutant, and the father of us all. There's 14 billion years crushed inside these pages, and most of them are pretty nasty.

Day of the Milkman by S. T. Cartledge

In a world dominated by the milk industry, only one milkman survives after a terrible storm sinks all the ships and throws the Great White Sea out of balance.

Moosejaw Frontier by Chris Kelso

An unapologetic disaster of metafiction

Notes from the Guts of a Hippo by Grant Wamack

A rugged journalist travels to Brazil in search of a missing hippo researcher and the notes left behind lead to something earth shatteringly revelatory.

Industrial Carpet Drag by Bruce Taylor

Chemicals make you do great things!

www.ingramcontent.com/pod-product-compliance
Lightning Source LLC
Chambersburg PA
CBHW022049170626
46808CB00003B/1416